D0581971

AUTUMN
PUBLISHING

Published in 2021
Published in the UK by Autumn Publishing
An imprint of Igloo Books Ltd
Cottage Farm, NN6 0BJ, UK
Owned by Bonnier Books
Sveavägen 56, Stockholm, Sweden
www.igloobooks.com

1221 001
2 4 6 8 10 9 7 5 3 1
ISBN 978-1-80108-108-5

Printed and manufactured in China

DUMBO GETS DRESSED

One morning, Mrs Jumbo gently wakes her little Dumbo.

"Are you ready for a big day under the Big Top?" she asks.

Dumbo looks at the pile of clothes in front of him. There are so many **shirts**, **trousers**, **hats** and **shoes**!

"Let's see," says Mrs Jumbo.
"What do you want to wear today?"
Dumbo looks at her and shrugs.

"Do you want to
dress up like a pirate
in a striped **shirt** and
fancy **coat**?" she asks.
"Pirates also wear **hats**
and **boots**."

Dumbo shakes his head.

"I love princess **dresses**," says Mrs Jumbo. "Would you like to dress like an elegant prince in a **suit** and **crown**?"

Dumbo shakes his head.

"What about a brave firefighter in a **red hat** and **yellow jacket**?" Mrs Jumbo asks.

Dumbo shakes his head.

"Okay," says Mrs Jumbo. "Maybe you'd like to dress like a cowboy. You'll need a **hat**, a **lasso** and a **bandana**!"

Dumbo shakes his head.

"Well," says Mrs Jumbo, "how about a brave knight with **armour**, a **sword** and a **shield**?"

Once again, Dumbo shakes his head.

"Let's see what else there is," says Mrs Jumbo. "Aha! I see a **cape**, a magic wand and a **top hat**. Do you want to be a magician?"

But Dumbo shakes his head.

"Hmmm," says Mrs Jumbo. "You could be a happy clown with polka-dot **trousers** and rainbow hair!"

One more time, Dumbo shakes his head.

"Oh, dear," says Mrs Jumbo. "I'm all out of ideas."

Mrs Jumbo picks up a familiar **yellow hat**. Dumbo smiles and nods!

"I see," Mrs Jumbo says happily. "You only want to wear your favourite **hat** and to be yourself today!"

D